PONY FRIENDS FOREVER

Meet all the ponies and find out more about the *Pony Friends Forever* series at

www.ponyfriendsforever.com

Pony Party

PAULINE BURGESS

First published in 2015
by Blackstaff Press
4D Weavers Court
Linfield Road
Belfast BT12 5GH

With the assistance of
The Arts Council of Northern Ireland

Supported by
The National Lottery®
through the Arts Council of Northern Ireland

arts
council
of Northern Ireland

Cover design by Anne Glenn Design
Cover and internal photographs by www.prime-photography.com

Typeset by KT Designs, St Helens, England
Printed in Berwick-upon-Tweed by Martins the Printers

A CIP catalogue record for this book is available from
the British Library

ISBN 978 0 85640 941 7

www.blackstaffpress.com

www.ponyfriendsforever.com

For Darcey, Tara and Emma
(the three musketeers)

Pony Friends
Forever

Welcome back to the Pony Palace and the third book in the *Pony Friends Forever* series. The books are inspired by a very special place – Lessans' Riding Stables near Saintfield, County Down, where my daughter Emma learned to ride. Though the people in my stories are fictional, all the horses and ponies in this series are real and have lived in the stables at one time or another.

In *Pony Party* you'll meet Gizmo, Daisy and Tonto, who have entertained us with their mischief and frolics over the years. I hope you enjoy reading their tales of fun, friendship and pony parties. Maybe you'll even find your new PFFs – Pony Friends Forever!

Pauline

OUTDOOR ARENA

INDOOR ARENA

YARD

NOSEBAG CAFE

OUTDOOR SEATING AREA

STABLES

Chapter One

GIZMO

Ah, I love strolling through the countryside! No 'change the rein at H' or 'jump those poles' – just breathing fresh air, swishing my merry little tail and going with the flow. Springtime hacks are my favourite part of living at the Pony Palace.

Of course the Pony Palace is just a riding school in County Down, not a *real* palace, but that's what we call it, and when some of the ponies around here act like precious princesses the name kind of makes sense.

I am, of course, referring to Miss Daisy, who is prancing along in front of me like the flower queen she thinks she is. She's everybody's favourite pony (or so she keeps telling me), whereas I'm what they call a bit of a plodder. It's not that I'm slow; I just like taking my own sweet time.

Our owner, Kate, calls me a daydreamer because most of the time I'm off in my own little Gizmo-world. I like to imagine that I'm living on the open plains of America, with the wind in my mane and not a care in the world. Kate lived in America for a while before she took over the Pony Palace, and I just *love* the sound of the place.

'Come on, boy. Walk on,' says Claire, who ends up riding me most of the time because she always arrives late and the 'popular' ponies are already taken by then.

'Really, Gizmo, if you were any slower you'd be going backwards,' she grumbles.

'Chillax, little girl,' I whinny. 'Why don't you take it easy and stop to smell the roses?' Well, daffodils in our case – that's what Kate calls the pretty yellow flowers growing along the lane.

Of course, Claire doesn't understand a word of my snorting, but I give my head a shake to try to make my point. Hurry, hurry, hurry, worry, worry, worry – that's all this little girl ever seems to do. She jumps out of her mum's car each week as if she's running to catch a train, then huffs and puffs as she grabs my tack and tells *me* off for making her late for the lesson! Maybe if she got here on time she could relax and actually enjoy the ride. But what do I know? I'm just a lazy old horse who likes to take things one day at a time.

'Come on, Gizmo, we're way behind the others!' Claire shouts.

'So what?' I think. 'We're not in the Grand National!' But Claire's life is one big race, so I reluctantly push myself into a trot and catch up with Daisy and Tonto. Claire is gripping

my sides so tightly with her legs that I feel like I'm wearing a girdle instead of a girth!

'This is supposed to be a hack,' I neigh. Definition of hack – riding a horse *gently* for *light* exercise.

'Are you okay at the back there, Claire?' Kate asks.

'Gizmo's just so stubborn, Kate,' she says. 'He won't budge. Please can I have a different pony next week?'

'He's not stubborn, he's just laid-back. Maybe you need to give him a bit more attention? Pat him, stroke him, let him know that you're his friend,' Kate says thoughtfully. 'Ponies need to know that you like them, and Gizmo's a sweetheart once he comes out of his dilly daydreams.'

'But I get bored with just walking around,' says Claire. 'I want to go faster! I'd love to be good enough to move up to the next class.'

Kate shakes her head, and I can't help thinking that Claire needs to take some time out of *Go, Go, Go* and try *Slow, Slow, Slow*! I'm going to have to teach her a thing or two about living life in the here and now. After all, today is a gift – that's why it's called the *present*!

Chapter Two

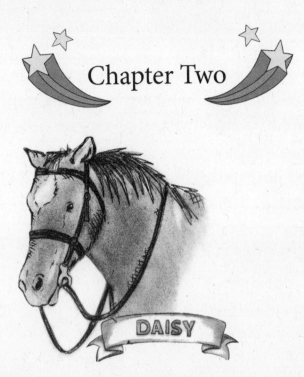

DAISY

That Gizmo is such a slowcoach. I had rather hoped we'd be riding together today, but, as usual, he's at least eight imaginary ponies behind me, and his poor rider is squeezing and kicking with all her might and he's still as slow as a snail. I, on the other hand, always do Exactly As I Am Told. Ask me to walk – I'll walk. Ask me to trot – I'll trot. Ask me to canter – well, you get the picture. Gizmo and Tonto call me a goody-goody, but what's so wrong with being well behaved? That's why Hannah picks me every week.

I've been at the Pony Palace for years and I've always been popular with the kids, but Hannah is my extra-special rider. She's seven-and-a-half and she's kind and funny and always brings me Polo mints. She wears the cutest riding hat you've ever seen – it's got lots of pretty stickers on it and letters stuck together that spell 'I love Daisy.' Not that I can read – I may be smart, but I'm *not* a genius.

'Good girl, Daisy,' Hannah says, and she reaches forward to give me a hug just before we join the Monlough Road. Her gran, Mrs Palmer, is walking alongside us on the hack –

she says it's good exercise, but I think she just likes to keep a close eye on Hannah. Hannah's mum works very hard and is always really busy, so Hannah spends a lot of time with her gran instead. Mrs Palmer says Hannah is the 'apple of her eye' – whatever that means. All I

know is that apples are the yummiest treat ever, so I guess humans love them just as much as ponies do.

My ears prick up as I hear a car approaching. Hannah pulls in tight to the side of the road behind the other riders, the car passes wide and slow, and Hannah and the others nod or wave to say thank you. Kate always says how important it is to respect other road users and to thank them when they show consideration.

Hannah is wearing a bright yellow vest so

she's easily spotted, but the countryside is so full of yellow right now she might as well be in camouflage: there are yellow blossoms on the gorse, yellow dandelions scattered through the fields and Kate's favourite – yellow daffodils. I'm lucky to live in a place like this, because I know there are horses out there who are not so well looked after and who don't live in such a beautiful place.

'Oh, I'm nearly out of puff,' Mrs Palmer is

saying. 'Maybe I should have just stayed in the Nosebag Café and had a wee cuppa.'

'Are you okay, Gran?' Hannah asks.

'Of course I am, lovey. I'm just not getting any younger,' she chuckles.

A few of the other parents have come out for the hack too, but they're all much younger than Hannah's gran. Her face is the colour of a ripe tomato with all this walking.

'Would you like me to walk you back, Mrs Palmer?' Mark asks. Mark is one of the older kids who helps out on Saturdays. He wants to run his own stables some day, so this is part of his training. 'Hannah will be fine on her own,' he says. 'Kate's at the front and there are plenty of volunteers around keeping an eye on the riders.'

Hannah's gran agrees and Mark checks that we're okay to ride along without them. He flashes a big white smile at Hannah and she giggles. I've heard some of the girls saying they've got something called a crush on Mark, whatever that means. He's such a nice lad, I hope they're not going to crush him to pieces! I can feel Hannah turning round to speak to Claire, who's finally getting closer to us.

'He is so cool!' Claire says, and Hannah just giggles some more. I give Gizmo a look to say 'giggling schoolgirls – what are they like?' but the dozy gelding just rolls his eyes and gazes into the distance. Back to his dilly daydreams!

Chapter Three

TONTO

Honestly, how do these humans expect us to trot along beside verges of juicy grass and *not* put our heads down for a bite? I am going to have this picnic whether my rider likes it or not. After all, they don't call me Tearaway Tonto for nothing!

My rider is shouting something in a language I don't understand. He tugs at my reins to tell me to lift my head, but this grass

is as sweet as honey and way too delicious
to ignore. Besides, I've never seen this boy
before, and I *don't* behave for strangers.
So I help myself, and it is yummy in my
tummy.

Ouch! Kate yanks my head up and scolds
me, then tells me to get a move on.

'He's just trying you out, Oskar,' she says to
my rider. 'Don't let him away with it – show
him who's boss.'

Well there's no mistaking who's boss around here, is there? Miss Kate Cooper, that's who! I decide to behave and trot along, but there had better be tasty hay in my stable when I get back …

Gizmo is walking ahead of me now, staring into goodness-knows-where while Daisy ogles him like he's a silver stallion. What *does* she see in him? Their riders are whispering and giggling like mad, but the boy on my back is silent. I think he must be new here. I give my head a shake to get his attention, but he thinks I'm being naughty again and tugs harder at my reins.

'Behave yourself!' he says, or at least that's what I think he says – he doesn't seem to be speaking the same language as the other kids. I sense that he's a bit nervous, so I decide to do as he asks and behave myself. We're off the road now, so Kate rides alongside us. We've done a kind of horseshoe-shaped hack and now we're heading back to the arena.

'That's right, Oskar. You have to be in control, otherwise Tonto will be in control of *you*. Is this your first hack?'

'Yes,' he answers shyly, and I can understand him this time, though he still sounds a bit funny. 'I did a little bit of riding in Poland, but I have wanted to take lessons since I came to Northern Ireland. My father rode a lot back home. I really want to be as good as him, but I don't think I ever will be.' He sounds really disappointed.

'Never compare yourself to someone else, Oskar. You have a nice seat, so that's a good start, and you have a good sense of balance. Just take it one day at a time and be yourself. You'll soon improve.'

Good old Kate! She's always giving advice to the riders. It's like she's everyone's mum, and even though she doesn't have any children

26

of her own, if you count all the riders that come to the Pony Palace every week, that's a *lot* of kids to be a stand-in mum to!

'How long have you lived in Belfast, Oskar?' she asks.

'Just a few months,' he answers. 'I like it here – except for the rain. It's always raining!'

Well that's just not true – the sun is shining right now, and the fields are bathed in a lovely golden glow. But he's right, of course, rain is a regular visitor to these parts, and thank goodness for that. Where would the tasty, green grass be without it?

'It will be my birthday soon,' Oskar tells

Kate. 'I would love to have a party, but I don't have many friends here.'

Kate puts her hand on his shoulder and

smiles. She leads us along the final part of the lane and from here I can see Kate's house and the rest of the farm. The tack room is just to the right and the stables and arenas are up ahead. It must be the last ride of the day, because Kate is telling all the riders to un-tack when they reach the yard and hand their ponies over to the volunteers. We must be going back up to the fields instead of the stables, which can only mean one thing: grass, grass and more grass. My tummy is rumbling already! When we get back the other riders are all chatting and laughing together, but Oskar just dismounts and walks away with his head down. I can't help but feel a bit sorry for him.

Chapter Four

GIZMO

Why *does* Daisy keep staring at me? I'm trying to imagine myself strolling through golden cornfields with the sun on my back, but she keeps distracting me with her big, brown eyes. Mark has got us all tacked up for a lesson in the indoor arena, and as he leads us out of the stable I can feel Princess Daisy watching me. Have I got flies on my tail or something?

I line up with eight other ponies in the arena and of course I'm the only one missing a rider. Then Claire runs in, pulling on her riding hat, late as usual. She mounts me without even checking my girth and gets a bit of a ticking-off from Kate.

'You know it's important to check your pony's girth, Claire,' she says. 'If it's not tight enough the whole saddle could swivel round, leaving you on the ground and me with an injured rider!'

'I'm sorry,' Claire mumbles. 'I was just in such a hurry …'

Mark comes over and tightens it for her. 'It's okay, Kate, I should have checked it for her anyway,' he says.

Claire thanks him, and I'm sure I detect a hint of adoration in her voice. Mark checks that everyone else is good to go and then Kate begins the lesson.

'We're going to start with some balance

exercises, then do some work on your steering,' she tells us. 'Claire, you lead the ride, please. Oskar to follow.'

One by one we all go large around the arena. The riders practise riding with one hand on the reins and one hand stretched out and moving in a circular motion. They practise with stirrups and without stirrups, then reach backwards to pat our docks and forwards to pat between our ears. Then Kate tells us all to do a figure of eight to check the riders' steering.

'Claire, tighten your reins, please,' she calls out. Claire is muttering something about being bored and wanting to go faster. I wish I could tell her to just relax a bit and enjoy the ride – it's *so* much more fun that way!

Kate tells us all to move forward into trot and that's when Claire seems happiest. She wants to learn to canter soon and I'm sure she'll love that, but I wish she'd realise how important the basics are too.

When we're finished and heading out of the arena Kate comes over to talk to Claire.

'You did well, Claire, but you need to give yourself more time before the lesson to prepare your pony properly. Why don't you try to get here twenty minutes early next week? That way you'll feel more relaxed and there'll be less rushing around at the last minute.'

Claire is standing beside me, holding my reins and staring at her feet. She looks a bit embarrassed. 'I know, I'm always in a rush. I just can't seem to arrive anywhere on time,' she mumbles.

'Your dad usually drops you off here, doesn't he?' Kate asks. 'How about I explain to him that it would be really good if you could arrive early for your lesson? I've even got a pony alarm clock I could lend you

until you get into the habit of waking up on time.'

'That would be great!' Claire replies, blushing. 'And if I do get here on time, can we start cantering in the fields and doing cross-country and things like that?'

'No, Claire!' Kate shakes her head. 'You're a good rider but you're nowhere near ready for cross-country. Gizmo is actually a really good pony for you – he's so calm that it kind of balances things out. Now, how about I treat you to a nice cold drink and we'll chat properly.'

Kate has worked her magic again. She's the best riding instructor ever, even if she does seem a little stern sometimes. Claire ties me up beside Daisy and heads off to the

Nosebag. I hear Mark telling her that he'll
help her tack up and get ready for the next few
lessons and her face bursts into the biggest,
widest smile. And now I have a delicious
half-hour of daydreaming ahead of me. Bliss.
The sun is shining over the Pony Palace, and
I'm imagining myself out on those wide-open
American prairies, ambling along and singing

a song, when I feel something tickling my neck …

'What are you *doing* Daisy?' I whinny. She moves her head closer to mine, and – OMG – she's nuzzling me! 'Get off, girl,' I'm tempted to say, but I don't want to be rude. And she *does* have those lovely brown eyes …

Chapter Five

DAISY

I wish Gizmo would look at *me* instead of staring into space all the time! I try nuzzling up to him, but he just backs off a bit and goes back to his dilly daydreams. Geldings can be *so* dim-witted sometimes!

Mark helped Hannah tie me up and now they're in the Nosebag waiting for Hannah's gran to pick her up. She's turning into such a good little rider, especially with Kate's encouragement, and it's really boosted her confidence. I'm glad about that, because sometimes I can sense that she feels quite sad that her mum never comes to watch her ride. I know she'd love her mum to see how well she does her rising trot now.

Tonto's trying to break away to reach some loose hay lying on the other side of the yard. He just never seems to stop eating!

'Stop it, Tonto!' I neigh, because I know he'll just get himself into trouble. Last night after the final ride he took himself down the fields to stuff his face with grass, and poor Kate had to run after him and tempt him back with some carrots. Honestly, he can be a menace sometimes.

'You'll be fed after the last ride,' I tell him. 'For goodness' sake, be patient.' He just snorts as if he's telling me to mind my own business.

A car pulls up at the yard and Hannah's

gran gets out. She walks very slowly up the little hill to the
Nosebag and seems to be panting a lot.

Hannah runs out excitedly and tells her all about the ride.

'Hello Mrs Palmer,' Kate says, walking over to them. 'Would you like a quick cup of tea or something?'

Kate has noticed what I've noticed: Mrs Palmer looks like she needs a sit down.

'Thank you, Kate. I'm not getting any younger and looking after a seven-year-old is a bit of a challenge at my age,' she laughs. But then she looks at Hannah so warmly that I can't imagine she minds at all.

'Hannah's mum works so hard to make sure this little one has everything she needs, but Hannah does miss spending time with her. Instead she gets stuck with me.'

'Well, she's lucky to have you, Mrs Palmer,' Kate says, leading her towards the café.

'Gran, can I just run over and give Daisy another hug while you're having your tea?' Hannah asks.

'Of course you can, lovey,' her gran replies.

Hannah wraps her arms around me and tells me all about a school trip she's going on soon. She says her class will be going to visit something called a horse sanctuary.

'The horses there have been neglected by their previous owners,' she says sadly. 'But they were rescued and now they're all being well looked after at the sanctuary. Some ponies just aren't as lucky as you guys here at the Pony Palace.'

I think about what she says for a minute. I've heard stories about horses not being taken care of properly and it makes me *so* angry. At least there are good people in the world who take them in and look after them.

'I wish I could save all the horses in the world. I'd make sure that none of them went hungry or got sick. In fact, that's what I want to do when I grow up,' she says, her face full of determination.

My lovely little Hannah – she really does have a heart of gold!

Chapter Six

TONTO

I didn't mean to make Kate chase me last night – I just couldn't resist the sight of all that lovely, long grass. Kate was really cross with me afterwards, though, and now Daisy's been telling me off too. The cheek of it! She's four years younger than me and yet she's bossing *me* around!

I look up and Oskar is heading in my direction with some yummy carrots. I thought he'd already gone home.

'Here,' he says, holding them out. 'For you.'

'Well, I don't mind if I do,' I neigh back. He feeds me four big, juicy carrots and I'm beginning to think that this boy might be all right. He rode me quite well in this evening's lesson and he was definitely keeping a tighter grip on my reins. Then I see Gizmo's rider, Claire, coming towards us.

'Hello,' Oskar says to her. 'Want to give some carrots to your pony?'

Oskar shares them with her and I'm *not* pleased. 'I thought those were for *me*!' I whinny.

'You rode really well today,' Claire is saying to him. 'You're always so calm. I seem to be in a permanent fluster.'

'I just like to take my time,' Oskar says to her. 'My grandmother always tells me not to wish my life away. I can't help wishing that I could have a proper birthday party this year, though. My friends are all in Poland, so I don't really know who to invite.'

'Haven't you made friends at school?' Claire asks. Oskar blushes a bit and looks away.

'Not really … I don't like to talk in class. Sometimes I forget words, and I am afraid no one will understand me.'

'I think your English is very good,' Claire says and, for the first time, Oskar gives a big, cheerful smile.

'I am very happy that I have found the Pony Palace,' he says. 'I have wanted to ride since I was a little boy. It is so good here.'

'I know, it's *so* much fun,' Claire says. 'Mind you, I still wish our lessons were more exciting, and that we could jump bounce fences or something.'

'I just want to get the basics right first,'

Oskar answers. 'My father always says it's important to learn the basic skills before you try more challenging things.'

Claire is nodding and looking at him as if he's got a point, but then Mark arrives to get us ponies ready for the last ride of the day and Claire turns her attention to him. Oskar looks a little disappointed, so I rub my head into his chest to make him feel a bit better.

'It's okay,' he says. 'I am used to being left out. I know people in Northern Ireland find me hard to understand sometimes, but I am

trying really hard, Tonto. I hope I will make some friends here soon.'

'I'll be your friend,' I neigh, and I nuzzle him a little bit more to prove it.

'Hey, what's going on, Tonto? You are being so nice to me today! Maybe you aren't such a naughty pony after all.'

Naughty? Me? Well, maybe a little – when there's yummy food around. I let Oskar stroke my nose and hope that he will start to feel like he fits in here. So what if his voice sounds a little different? So what if he comes from a different country? As a wise horse once neighed, 'Why fit in when you were born to stand out?'

Chapter Seven

GIZMO

The kids are mucking out our stables today as part of their lesson. Kate says it's important for them to learn about all aspects of looking after ponies, including cleaning out our stalls.

Claire was actually here on time for a change and she seems to be having good fun poo-picking in my stable. There's no accounting for taste, is there?

Oskar is helping her, and those two look like they're becoming proper friends.

'Oy!' I snort, as a heap of straw goes flying over my head. I know I wanted Claire to try and chillax a bit, but I didn't expect her to play hay fights with me as piggy-in-the-middle! She's supposed to be putting my old bedding into a wheelbarrow, not throwing it at Oskar.

When they're finished monkeying around

Claire sweeps the stable floor clean before shaking down some clean straw.

Oh, it's going to be so comfy in there tonight. Hours of lovely dreaming ahead!

'Now, Gizmo, let's get you cleaned up,' she says. For some reason the kids just love grooming us, and I must say, there are worse things in life than being gently brushed and beautified.

Claire picks my hooves and gets rid of all my loose hair with a currycomb. My thick winter coat is dropping off bit by bit, and my new glossy, grey coat is beginning to shine through. I imagine myself with flowers in my mane and green grass under my hooves, glistening in the American sunshine …

'Hi Claire,' Hannah says, walking towards us. 'I need the hose to wash Daisy, but I'm not sure where it is.'

'Come on, I'll help you look,' Claire replies. They find the hose and start to spray Daisy, while Olivia, one of the volunteers, gives them instructions.

'Don't spray the pony's face or get water in her ears,' she tells them. 'When you're finished hosing, sponge her down gently.'

The girls do exactly as they are told and then it's my turn for a lovely cool shower. The water trickles down my shoulders and onto my back and it's as refreshing as a spring breeze.

'Don't you just love Saturdays at the Pony Palace?' Claire asks as she sponges my back.

'Defo,' says Hannah. 'And I love seeing Daisy. She's my PFF.'

I'm wondering what Claire will say, because

I know I am definitely *not* her PFF, but to my surprise she says, 'I know exactly what you mean. Gizmo used to kind of get on my nerves because he can be a bit slow, but he's a cutie really. *And* he can go into a good trot when you ask him nicely. I think I'm finally getting the hang of him,' she says.

'I'm getting the hang of you too, Claire,' I whinny. She's so much more fun when she's not in a rush all the time. Maybe she's finally learning how to take it easy and go with the flow.

'I wonder who that is?' Claire says suddenly, looking up. A very tall, thin lady is walking towards the stables.

Hannah looks puzzled. 'It's my mum,' she says. 'I wonder why she's here?'

Hannah runs towards her and I can't hear what the lady is saying, but Hannah starts to cry. I hate to see any of the kids upset, and Claire must be sad about it too, because she runs over and gives Hannah the biggest, warmest hug. I wonder what on earth is wrong?

Chapter Eight

DAISY

My poor Hannah. She cried floods of tears this afternoon when her mum arrived and told her that her gran was sick. Mrs Palmer had a pain in her heart and had to go to hospital in an ambulance.

It must be a scary thing, because hearing about it really upset Hannah. I stood in the yard trying to make sense of it all, but it was hard to understand with Hannah sobbing so much.

'You'll have to leave your lesson early and come with me, pet,' Hannah's mum said.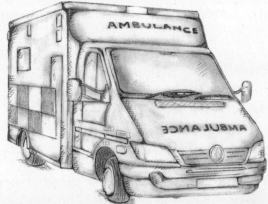

'We'll go check on Gran and then I'll take you home.'

'Is Gran going to be okay, Mum?'

'I'm sure she will, love. But in the meantime you'll have to give up your lessons. We need to spend time with Gran in the hospital.'

Poor Hannah looked as miserable as I felt. Her gran is ill, and on top of that she won't even get to see me! It just isn't fair. Gizmo's rider Claire was trying to cheer Hannah up with cuddles and kind words, and Kate was doing her best, as always, to make things better.

'Your gran is in the best possible place at the minute, Hannah,' Kate said. 'The doctors will do all they can to make her well, and she'll be back with you in no time. And don't worry about Daisy – we'll look after her until you're ready to come back.'

I watched Hannah go off with her mum and my heart felt like it was breaking. She's the nicest rider I've ever had and I hate to see her so upset. Now I'm out here in the field grazing and I miss her already.

It's a beautiful April evening and even though the countryside looks lovely I just can't lift my spirits. There are grassy, green hills rolling into one another all the way to Saintfield, the sky is pale blue and the Mourne Mountains look like a purplish ridged roof in the distance, but all I can see are the weeks without Hannah.

Suddenly, I feel someone nuzzling me. Gizmo is nudging my face and making soft, low sounds. He tells me not to worry – which isn't so easy – and that everything will be all right. Then we stand and gaze out over the fields around us as the sun sets, and just having him there beside me makes me feel a little bit better. I know how lucky I am to be here, at home with my family of horses and humans, and I just wish Hannah could have her gran at home with her right now.

Humans don't think we ponies remember our mothers, but we do. When I had to leave my family to come and live at the Pony Palace I sniffed around after her for days. I was so sad at first, but I got used to it, because that's what it's like in the horse world.

It's different for humans, though; they don't leave their families until they're all grown up, so poor Hannah must be devastated to be without her gran right now. I can't wait to see her again and give her the biggest, sloppiest nuzzle in the whole world. I just don't know when that will be.

Chapter Nine

TONTO

We spent the night out in one of the fields last night because the weather's starting to get warmer, and I was in heaven munching on all that grass.

Daisy seemed a bit quiet, though. She must really be missing her favourite rider, because she didn't even poke her nose in to tell me to stop eating so much. Gizmo was keeping a close eye on her, which is not like him. He's normally in cloud cuckoo land!

Oskar is coming to the Pony Palace again today. I was thinking what a good idea it would be for him to have his birthday party here, but of course I have no way of telling him that. The parties here always look like great fun. The kids get lots of delicious food in the Nosebag after their rides, and Kate gives out special rosettes to the birthday groups.

I wish *I* could squeeze my way into the Nosebag and sniff out some of those lovely sandwiches. Yum, yum – I can almost taste them!

Oskar arrives then and walks over to me, looking a bit down in the dumps.

'Hi Tonto,' he says quietly. I give him a nuzzle and hope that there are some carrots hiding in his pockets, but he just sighs and stares off into the distance.

'What's wrong?' I neigh, and he answers as if he understands me.

'My mum and dad say there is no point in me having a party this year. They say I should wait until next year when I know more people,' he says sadly.

He sighs again and strokes my shoulder. 'They're probably right,' he adds. 'I still haven't made any friends at school. Who would want to come to my party?'

I feel really sorry for him, and suddenly I understand why Daisy's so upset about her rider. We spend so much time with these humans – I guess we get kind of close to them.

Oskar tacks me up with Kate's help, but it doesn't feel like he even wants to ride today.

I do my best to spur him on and give him a fun morning that will take his mind off things.

Kate gets us to trot around poles and ride in and out of the serpentine. Some of the other riders look like blobs of jelly bouncing up and down, but Oskar has the hang of the rising trot now and gets into a nice, steady rhythm. I can sense that he's cheering up a bit and I do my best not to spook or put my head down suddenly or do anything that would make him lose his balance. His dad is watching from the viewing gallery and giving him a thumbs up.

'Well done, Oskar!' his dad shouts.

Afterwards, when Oskar goes to the Nosebag to get a cold drink, I overhear his dad speaking to Kate. He's telling her how worried he was about Oskar learning to speak English and settling into a new school when they moved to Northern Ireland.

'It can't have been easy,' Kate says. 'But he's a good lad and he always tries his best. His English is improving, and he seems to have really taken to riding here.'

'Yes, he fits in here,' Oskar's dad says. 'He doesn't say much about school, though, and I have a feeling that he hasn't made many friends there yet. It's his birthday soon and he wants to have a party, but what if he invites people and they say no? Then Oskar would be really upset.'

Kate goes quiet for a minute or two, and I can tell that she has her thinking cap on.

'Why doesn't he have his party here?' she asks. 'After all, he's really settled in well. He's made friends with some of the other riders, and a party is a great way to get to know people. It could be a surprise for him. Just leave the inviting to me.' Kate seems determined to put her plan in place.

Oskar's dad looks really grateful. He thanks Kate for helping his son to feel like a part of the Pony Palace.

I think about this as they head off. When I first arrived at the Pony Palace I didn't know anyone and I felt a bit nervous – I suppose everyone does when they're new. The other horses and ponies soon made me feel at home and became my friends, even if they did think I was a teeny bit greedy. Maybe I should give some of that friendship back now and go talk to Daisy. She's obviously upset, and I've been too busy munching to bother helping her. I think it's time I showed some team spirit – after all, that's what PFFs do.

Chapter Ten

GIZMO

Daisy's been so upset about Hannah. I tried to cheer her up, and I think it helped a bit, but I couldn't believe it when even Tearaway Tonto started being really nice to her last Sunday morning. He actually stopped thinking about eating long enough to consider someone's feelings! At first I thought pigs might fly, but there's no chance of the resident pig here *ever* getting up from that soft pile of straw he sleeps on.

Claire arrived in plenty of time this morning to get me tacked up and ready for business. Her dad drops her off earlier now and it makes such a difference. She's less flustered and much more easy-going. We're starting to make quite a team! Kate's always telling the kids how important it is to build a relationship with their horses, so I'm glad that Claire works with me now, not against me.

'Ready, Gizmo? We're out in the sand school today,' Claire says, leading me towards the outdoor arena. I love riding there because you can see right down the hills and across the fields. We trot over poles and do a few low jumps and I can tell that Claire is really enjoying herself.

Kate decides to let her try something more challenging and go for an even higher jump. Claire seems really excited as she turns me around and angles me towards the jump. Off we go in sitting trot and then into a canter. Up, up, up and over! Yes, we manage it! But wait, what's Claire doing on the ground? She's lying in the sand, covered in dust and muck, and I think my heart actually stops beating for a second. Then I hear Claire's voice and let out a big sigh of relief.

'Sorry, Kate,' she calls out. 'I just lost my balance.'

Phew! She sounds okay, thank goodness, though she does look a bit shocked.

'Next time you're going over a higher jump, hold on to Gizmo's mane until you get the hang of it,' Kate says.

'I will. Maybe I wasn't quite ready for that yet. I guess I *should* just stick to the basics for now.'

Kate nods her head as if to say, 'I told you so.' Then she brushes the sand off Claire and checks that she's okay. The kids are used to

the occasional fall, and as long as they're not
hurt Kate tells them to get right back on. That
way they won't lose their confidence. I'm
proud of Claire. She just gets up, wipes out
her sandy mouth with a tissue, and off we go
again.

'You're only a real horse rider after your
first fall,' Kate tells her afterwards, and it's
true.

Of course, we don't mean to throw our riders off – sometimes things just go a bit wonky. I'm hoping Claire isn't cross with me, but she soon puts me at ease when she gives me a lovely, snuggly goodbye hug.

'That's my girl,' I neigh back to her. 'Live, learn and make some mistakes – that's what life is all about.'

And then I suddenly realise how happy I am to be here, nuzzling my favourite rider and gazing off into the County Down countryside, and I think that maybe I don't need American prairies to be happy after all. Maybe the Pony Palace will do just as well.

Chapter Eleven

DAISY

Hannah hasn't been able to make it to the Pony Palace all week. In fact, I heard Kate say that she might not be coming back at all. Even though Gizmo and Tonto are being really nice to me, I just can't seem to cheer up. I have lots of other lovely riders – Darcey, Tara, Emma and many more – but Hannah is kind of special. I know her voice, her smell, her laughter – everything. I don't even feel like being part of a ride today.

Gizmo comes trotting back into the stables full of excitement. He tells me all about the lesson in the sand school and how Claire fell off. I've noticed that he's a lot more animated lately and spends less time dilly daydreaming.

'She's okay, though,' he tells me. 'The sand school's pretty soft, so she didn't hurt herself, and she got right back on afterwards.'

It's nice to see Gizmo taking an interest in his rider. Claire's been good for him, and Oskar's been really good for Tonto. But what about me? All the other kids here are great, but they're just not Hannah.

'Hello there, Daisy,' Kate says, walking towards me. 'Sophie's going to be riding you this afternoon, so Mark will be along soon to tack you up.'

'I don't want anyone else to ride me,' I whinny sadly. Besides, Sophie normally rides

Parsley. She's used
to riding at a
different pace.

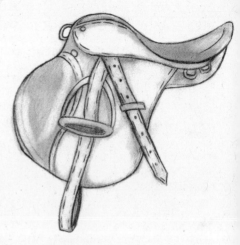

Kate must
understand me
because she says
that Sophie needs
to try out other
horses.

'Partnerships are good, but it's important
for riders to try out other ponies – just like
it's important for you ponies to adapt to other
riders,' she says. 'Anyway, I don't want you in
here in the stable moping all day. Much better
to get you outside into the fresh air.'

'Oh, all right then,' I nicker. Sophie is a
sweet little girl, and maybe the lesson will take
my mind off things. Old Rupert in the next
stable gives me a nod and tells me to get out
there and enjoy myself. Rupert's retired now
and he always gives us younger ponies good

advice. So when Mark comes in I let him lead me out and put my best hoof forward. After all, *all* the riders at the Pony Palace are special, and they deserve a pony who's on top form.

Chapter Twelve

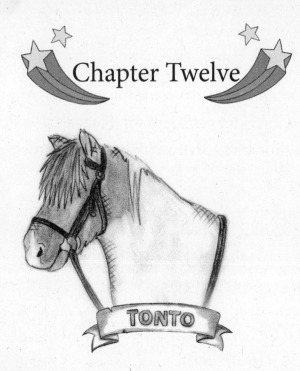

TONTO

Now you're talking! We're trekking through the countryside and, believe it or not, I'm allowed to put my head down as much as I want! We're having a treasure hunt and I'm actually *supposed* to bury my head in the grass, to look for treasure.

'I found another one!' Oskar shouts. Each rider has to find eight different coloured horseshoes along the bridle paths and in the fields. Then they get to go back to the Nosebag for a big surprise. I wonder what it could be ...

Oskar dismounts and picks up a yellow horseshoe hidden in a clump of daffodils, then calls over to Claire. 'How many have you got?'

'Six,' she shouts back. 'What about you?'

'Seven! Only one more to go,' he replies.

Mark walks behind us, collecting the horseshoes from the riders and keeping a record as he goes along. Claire waves and beams at him, but then she turns to Oskar and gives him an even bigger smile. Those two seem like really good friends now.

A little while later, Oskar whispers to me that today is actually his birthday. He says that he's a bit

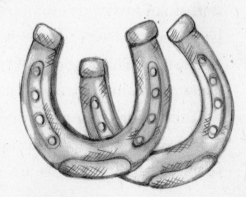

sad that he's not having a party, but that he's having good fun on the hack today anyway.

'Never mind, Oskar,' I whinny back to him. 'Sometimes life is just like that. We don't always get exactly what we want, and sometimes you just have to go with the flow …' Uh oh, I'm starting to sound like Gizmo!

We can hear lambs baaing across the fields as we trot around looking for more treasure. There are yellow flowers in the hedgerows that look like shiny little butter clusters, and I can hear sparrows cheeping above my head. Oskar is chatting happily to me and I realise I can understand what he's saying – in both of his languages. I also realise that I've really started to like him. He's a good, strong rider who knows what he wants and I respect that.

Then I hear Kate say, 'First one back to the Nosebag with eight horse shoes gets a special surprise!' and before I know it our riders are jumping off our backs and scampering around like baby goats.

Claire finds two more coloured horseshoes but Oskar finds his faster. He jumps on my back as quick as he can and trots me back to the yard.

'Am I the winner?' he asks Kate.

'You certainly are, Oskar!' she replies. 'Would you like to see your special surprise now?'

She leads him into the Nosebag, which is decorated from top to bottom with birthday banners and balloons. Oskar's mum and

dad are there and so is Hannah and even Mrs Palmer! All the volunteers and loads of the other riders are there and they all start singing, 'Happy Birthday to you …'

Oskar looks gobsmacked. Olivia and Mark lead us ponies right into the yard outside the café so we can see everything that's going on, and Daisy's ears move forward with delight when she spots Hannah. Claire comes trotting up behind us on Gizmo and dismounts to give Oskar the biggest birthday hug ever.

'Your dad told me that you wanted to have a birthday party,' Kate explains. 'So I hope you're as pleased as we are to celebrate it at the Pony Palace. We organised the treasure hunt to get you out of the way while we got everything ready.'

Oskar's eyes look a bit glossy, but he has a huge smile on his face. He looks all around him at everyone in the Nosebag and seems

really surprised when he sees three boys
sitting on the big green sofa.

'I invited some of your friends from school,'
his dad says. 'They're really keen to learn all
about horse riding.'

The Nosebag is full of happy people who all
want to share Oskar's day.

'What do you think, son?' his mum asks.

'I think this is the best birthday ever!' he
replies.

'Just one more thing,' says Kate. 'We haven't given you your present yet.'

Kate turns Oskar towards the yard and tells him he can have a pony on loan for a whole day.

'It will be just like owning your own horse for the day,' she smiles. 'It's yours to ride, groom, and have fun with. Who would you like to choose?'

She points to all of us tethered in the yard: Barney, Biscuit, Parsley, Gizmo, Skippy, Daisy, Dury ... and then Oskar looks at me.

'Please may I have the greediest, cheekiest pony in the Pony Palace,' he says, beaming. 'Tearaway Tonto.'

'Sure?' asks Kate.

'Sure!' says Oskar.

And inside I'm thinking that I will never, ever stop for a picnic again when Oskar is riding me. No more escaping into the fields for juicy grass, and no more thinking that

I'm the boss when I've got a kid on my back. I'm so proud to be chosen as Oskar's special pony that I decide to be As Good As Gold like Daisy from now on. And who should nuzzle me at that very moment but Princess Daisy herself. Little Hannah and her gran are standing beside her, and Mrs Palmer looks as healthy as an April afternoon.

'Hi Oskar, hi Claire,' Hannah says happily. 'I've really missed being here, but Gran's much better now so I'm back for good. And I'm extra, extra pleased to be here for your party.'

Daisy looks like she's on top of the world and I'm so glad that her favourite rider is back at the Pony Palace.

'That's brilliant,' says Claire. 'We've missed you, Hannah. Haven't we Oskar?'

And Claire smiles at Oskar, the birthday boy, and then his classmates walk over and suddenly Oskar is surrounded by friends.

And do you know what happens next?

Gizmo strolls over to Daisy, lowers his head, pushes his ears forward and touches Daisy's nose with his. They stand like that for ages, just gazing at each other, and I think to myself how everything in life is better when you can share it with friends. Even food!

Then the music starts blasting from inside the Nosebag and all the kids start dancing like puppets on strings. Well, you know what they say: if you can't beat them – join them! So Daisy and Gizmo and all us ponies start to boogie-woogie our little hind legs off and it's just THE BEST PONY PARTY EVER!

The End

Fact Files

Name	Gizmo
Colour	Grey
Height	12.2 hh
Loves	Daydreaming
Hates	Rushing

Name	Daisy
Colour	Black
Height	12.2 hh
Loves	Gizmo
Hates	Bad behaviour

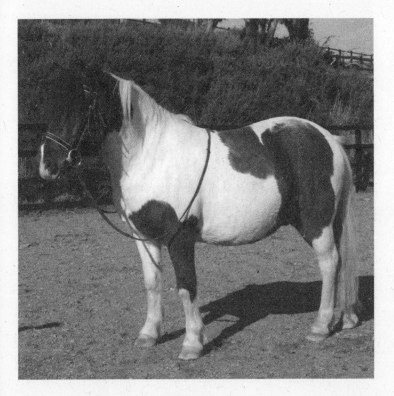

Name	Tonto
Colour	Skewbald (white and brown)
Height	12.2 hh
Loves	Picnics
Hates	Being hungry!

Acknowledgements

I would like to thank Philippa Auret, Ruth, Nicky, Manus, Bethany, Laura and all who help out at Lessans Riding Stables week after week.

I am indebted to Ann and Tom at the Nosebag Café for their generous hospitality and the best sausage butties in County Down, as well as all the parents and grandparents who share food and friendship with my family and me every Saturday.

Thank you to all at Blackstaff Press and to Damian Smyth at the Arts Council of Northern Ireland, for their faith in my stories.

And finally, to my family and friends, thank you so, so much for supporting me on my writing journey.

More from the
Pony Friends Forever series

Book One

eBook
EPUB ISBN 978-0-85640-580-8
KINDLE ISBN 978-0-85640-598-3

Paperback
ISBN 978-0-85640-923-3

www.blackstaffpress.com

Pony Friends Forever
Book Two

eBook
EPUB ISBN 978-0-85640-662-1
KINDLE ISBN 978-0-85640-680-5

Paperback
ISBN 978-0-85640-936-3

www.blackstaffpress.com